MAX HELPS OUT

by Linda Apolzon Neilson
illustrated by Dorothy M. Stott

A GOLDEN BOOK • NEW YORK

Western Publishing Company, Inc. Racine, Wisconsin 53404

On Saturday Max's father takes him to the hardware store. The hardware store sells paint and paint brushes, nails, saws, hammers, screwdrivers, and many other things.

Today Max and his dad want sandpaper, a tube of caulking, and a can of blue paint.

Max and Dad choose just the right color blue. The clerk fastens the can onto a machine that shakes and shakes the paint to mix it up.

When they get back home, Max carries the bag with
the caulking and the sandpaper inside. He follows Dad
to the empty room where nobody sleeps.

Mamma is there, holding a scraper. She uses it to scrape old, chipped paint off the window frame.

Dad fits the tube of caulking into his caulking gun. Then he squeezes the caulking onto the wall in a zigzag line. It looks like toothpaste. Dad runs his finger over the caulking to smooth it.

Max runs his finger over it, too.

"This is how we patch cracks in the wall," Dad says.

"Did you buy some sandpaper?" asks Mamma.

"I'll get it!" says Max.

Mamma tears off a piece of sandpaper and rubs it
back and forth on the window frame. This makes
the bumpy places smooth. She gives Max a piece
of sandpaper, and he sands the window frame, too.

Dad brings a drop cloth into the empty room.
Max helps to spread it out. The drop cloth keeps
paint off the floor.

Dad pours paint into a pan. He rolls a paint roller through it, soaking up paint.

Sweep! Sweep! Dad rolls paint on the wall
in broad strips of blue.

Mamma uses a small brush to paint the
window frame. She paints slowly, carefully,
along each edge.

Later, when the paint is dry, Dad brings a shiny new doorknob into the empty room.

He chooses the right screwdriver to fasten the doorknob in place. Max hands him the screws.

"Now the closet door closes," says Dad.

Mamma opens out a folding ruler and measures the wall. She makes a tiny pencil mark.

Tap! Tap! With a hammer Dad carefully taps a nail into the wall.

Mamma hangs a picture on the nail. Then she smiles.

Max and Dad look at the picture and the blue walls and smile, too.

Look! The room is not empty any more. Someone is sleeping there. It's Max. This is his room now. Good night, Max.